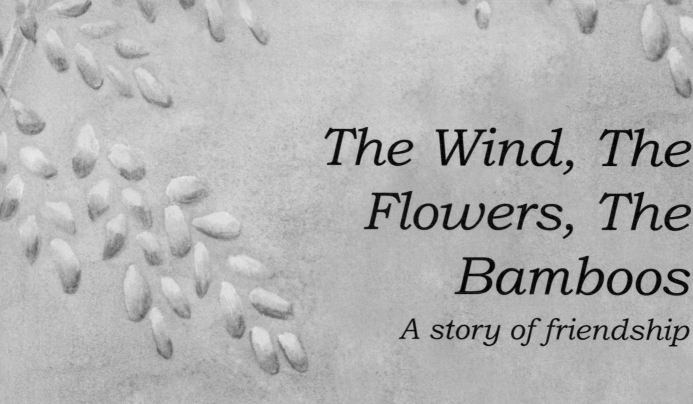

The Wind, The Flowers, The Bamboos

A story of friendship

written by Sally Lake-Dolejsi

Archway Publishing books may be ordered through booksellers or by contacting:

Archway Publishing
1663 Liberty Drive
Bloomington, IN 47403
www.archwaypublishing.com
844-669-3957

Interior Image Credit: Karla Browder-Little

ISBN: 978-1-6657-1214-9 (sc)
ISBN: 978-1-6657-1215-6 (hc)
ISBN: 978-1-6657-1216-3 (e)

Print information available on the last page.

Archway Publishing rev. date: 10/6/2021

ARCHWAY
PUBLISHING

AUTUMN

The crisp Autumn wind was blowing through the woodlands with citrus and floral scents as Mrs. Owl set off to search for some lemons and chrysanthemums for a very special occasion!

It was a very special day indeed! Not only was it the monthly gathering of the neighborhood ladies for a game of mahjong, but it was also Mrs. Field Mouse's birthday! Oh my! Mrs. Owl tightened the laces of her bonnet and went about gathering more lemons and flowers for the big day!

Mrs. Owl stopped at Mrs. Turtle's famous lemon garden to gather the best of the fruit. Mrs. Turtle always had so many to give away! The two chatted and then Mrs. Owl gave Mrs. Turtle a hug goodbye as there was so much to do!

Back at the Owl home, Mrs. Owl was busy cooking and baking. There were puddings, tarts and parfaits being made and of course, the big birthday cake decorated with lemon slices!

Mrs. Owl decorated the home with big balloons and floral arrangements in yellows and green and placed parfaits around the mahjong table where the ladies would be playing.

The cake was also ready with candles waiting to be lit!

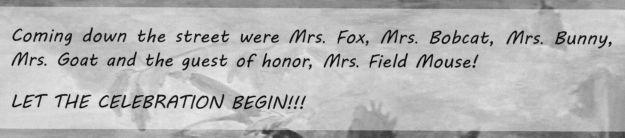

Coming down the street were Mrs. Fox, Mrs. Bobcat, Mrs. Bunny, Mrs. Goat and the guest of honor, Mrs. Field Mouse!

LET THE CELEBRATION BEGIN!!!

The room had a large birthday banner, and all the desserts and flowers were set on the pretty table. The ladies were all laughing and having such a marvelous time! Mrs. Fox was even dancing on a chair!

As the evening came to an end, it was obvious everyone had enjoyed themselves.... maybe a little too much as their tummies were aching from all those parfaits and tarts!

WINTER

As the months passed, the days were getting shorter, and the wind blew much cooler through the trees. Snow was gently falling, and the families of the woodlands nestled in for the long months ahead.

OWL

Even though it was cold outside, Mr. and Mrs. Owl cozied up next to the outdoor fireplace that was glowing with warm orange and yellow flickering lights. They wrapped a blanket around them and sipped on some warm wassail and were thankful for the quiet and calm of just being together.

Mrs. Field Mouse was busily decorating the Christmas tree while Mr. Field Mouse was putting naughty elves in secret places! The house was cheery and bright and full of laughter!

Meanwhile, over at the Fox home, the sound of a sewing machine was buzzing. Mrs. Fox always made the most beautiful pillows during Christmas to give to her friends! Mr. Fox observed while quietly reading his book by a warm fire inside.

The smell of spice was in the air over at the home of Mr. and Mrs. Bobcat. Mr. Bobcat was preparing his famous bottles of spice for the season while Mrs. Bobcat wrapped presents and sang Christmas carols.

Everyone was enjoying the quiet company in their own homes until that time came again for the ladies to get together for their monthly mahjong game.

Mahjong was held at the home of Mrs. Goat this time. Even though it was winter, all the ladies could not resist the homemade ice cream she always made! Pecan praline! Again, there was loud laughter and Mrs. Bunny and Mrs. Fox nearly fell off their seats they were laughing so much!

As the evening came to a close, the ladies were feeling a little woozy from too much ice cream and laughter

SPRING

The sun started to peek overhead as the melting snow gave way to tiny wildflowers that started to pop up from the ground. Soon all that lay quiet over the last few months started to waken and emerge in the woodlands. It was Spring!

Mr. and Mrs. Field Mouse were outside trimming bushes and hedges and adding sunflowers to the home. Mrs. Field Mouse was quite the gardener!

Next door, Mrs. Fox brought her paint brushes outside to capture the emerging wildflowers. Mr. Fox was also outside working on some wooden flower boxes for Mrs. Fox.

The Bobcat home was busy with the building of a new outdoor area that included a large farm table and seating under a tree. Perfect for the neighborhood get togethers that always happened during the Spring and Summer!

Meanwhile, at the Owl home, Mrs. Owl was reaching up to a tree limb to hang a new wind chime when a cold and unexpected breeze blew her out of the yard!

The wind continued to blow her so deep into the forest and out of the woodlands, she found herself alone and scared. The surroundings were not familiar, and it became very dark.

Out of the shadows, Mrs. Owl saw Mrs. Fox, Mrs. Bobcat and Mrs. Field Mouse emerging. They gently gathered Mrs. Owl and helped her back to the woodlands and home.

Mrs. Owl was experiencing loss and sadness, but her friends remained at her side and surrounded her with love, friendship and comfort.

Every day, the ladies would come visit Mrs. Owl and bring her hot soup and gifts of flowers and treats to cheer her up and make sure she healed. Slowly Mrs. Owl began to feel much better.

SUMMER

As Mrs. Owl got stronger and was able to get around better, she walked around her home and noticed it felt too big and empty now that she was alone. She looked at pictures of her family and thought about her children.

With a heavy heart, Mrs. Owl packed up her belongings from her home and decided it was time to move nearer to her children so she could be surrounded by family and comfort once again.

The moving wagon was loaded up with Mrs. Owl and her boxes and the neighborhood ladies came by to wave goodbye. There were tears shed but also much love and friendship.

Upon arriving at her children's place, there was much joy and hugs and plenty of love surrounding Mrs. Owl and her family

Mrs. Owl thoughtfully placed her personal belongings in their place of her new little cottage next door to her children. There were flowers, fruits, nuts and all the things that she cherished before. Joy sprung in her heart!

Mrs. Owl spent her days baking and cooking treats for her family, and they often came to eat and celebrate the memories of all the loved ones they held close to their hearts.

One day in the mail, there was a lovely little card that arrived! Mrs. Owl's friends from the Woodlands announced a special Mahjong evening! Oh joy! What a fun visit lay ahead for Mrs. Owl!

Mrs. Owl baked special mahjong cookies and loaded up her suitcase for the visit!

When Mrs. Owl arrived, Mrs. Field Mouse had her home full of treats, flowers and oh, what an evening of mahjong, friendship, love and laughter!!